ANCIENT ONES

Timothy Hargreaves

Willows West

ISBN: 979-8-9998695-4-8

Cover design by: Timothy Hargreaves

Printed in the United States of America

This earth holds a memory

of lives that have passed.

Step softly.

The rocks bear

their signs,

the lives they once lived.

Remember.

LIFE

Time and place that merge into memory

NOW THEY WERE THREE.

The moaning held low, pulled from deep inside. She crouched in the corner, hands reaching for the roof of the cave, toes curled and gripping the earthen floor. The boy stayed away. His monotone chanting, soft and gentle, rising and falling with the intensity of the girl's guttural sound. His eyes didn't move from the ground as he prayed to appease the ancestors.

The screams came. Shattering the night like the sound of the wolf as it reached out over the canyon to its mate. The boy tightened his fingers, rolling them into fists, but keeping them close, held to his side. He called out too. Reaching down below the earth. Reaching down to say, we are here, we do not disrespect you. We bring life.

The silence held for a moment. The girl's breathing—quick and urgent, slowing as she sank back, easing to the ground. She reached forward, grasping for the child, cradling it to her. The boy waited, arms

1

raised, and fingers splayed wide. The child writhed once then cried out, mewing loud and hard. The boy had stopped chanting. The ancestors knew this sound. The call of life. A cry to its mother, to the world.

I am here.

Across the barranca, the sun brushed the rim of the canyon wall on the east facing buttress.

Morning.

He would gather the food. But later. Now he stayed, creeping closer to the girl and the child with quiet steps, his hands reaching forward to touch. The girl raised her head, her dark hair slicked and close to her face—her dark eyes settling on his, remaining, unbroken.

His touch was light and he moved gently. The girl reached down and presented him with the knife. A stone tool, chipped to a keen edge that she used on the skins of the mule deer and the sheep. He took it deliberately, gripping tightly to the helve of the stone blade.

He smoothed the slick on the child's head once, pausing to feel the warmth and slow contented movements as it suckled the girl. His hand moved surely, and he sliced the connection between the girl and the child.

She nodded once.

It was done.

This new life, now connected to this place.

The boy placed the knife back with her belongings and worked his way out of the wall house and onto the ledge. His vision moved outward—searching unconsciously for anything that spoke of change. Early morning was the time for animals. He caught the sway of a branch that could be game. Overhead the crow circled lazily, cawing to its family and the canyon walls.

The woodpile leaned against the stone cliff. He grabbed some twigs that had washed down an arroyo. They were dry enough for the fire. His hands worked—snapping the sticks with rough care, before he turned back to the house.

He fed the fire, then turned for a pot. His gaze strayed to the girl with the child in her arms. Both asleep, close to the corner, crawled away from the blood. He would take it to the crack in the rock for the ancestors after he got water.

That night the moon rose sharp and full—light casting nighttime shadows through the still canyon, beams landing in the wall house, as the boy and girl ate slowly. They sat tight together on fresh rushes he'd collected that day.

The girl had slept, then woken, then slept again.

The boy had worked—brought water, bedding, and some corn. Each time he returned, he watched for any change in the girl or the child.

As he finished his last bite, the girl lifted the child and extended her arms toward him. He leaned in, his arms curling forward to meet her, accepting the child, he pulled it close, breathing in a smell of the new thing.

He wrapped the child tighter, leaned back, and closed his eyes.

LEAVING

When all is done, we start again

THE BOY DESCENDED LIGHTLY to the canyon floor, knees and ankles absorbing the shock from the last small drop—a motion practiced since childhood. He touched a knee to the worn grit of the sandy floor, then, in a smooth motion, stood tall, hands at his sides, chin raised.

He lifted his gaze up to the dwellings, up to the people. They gazed back—heads tilted low to keep him in view. He brushed the sling that held the pot, the seeds—corn and squash, and his tools for fire. He moved the atlatl to his left hand, raising his right in a final gesture of farewell, without regret.

The people watched, expressionless as the sheer walls of the buttes that surrounded them. At last, he saw his sister raise a hand. She called out: *good hunting, good life, I'll miss you.*

The boy turned and walked away. Away to a new life. Away from the people—the people who grew too many.

It would take him two days to reach the new place.

A place remembered.

His father had shown him: *see that ledge? It lived before.* The stones still stood from abandoned granaries. A time before, when people had descended from the mesa because of hunger, or drought, or both.

But it had been the boy who had noticed the seep. Close to the ledge—possibly reachable. Water that would drip all year. Water—even in the dry season.

He picked his way across a dry wash, thick with debris from a recent flood. Boulders and stones, the limbs of trees. Here and there a tree trunk. Dense bushes hindered his path occasionally. But he moved around or pushed through—whatever was easiest. His path out of the canyon climbed gently over grey and silver bands of familiar rock, the sediment gripping his bare feet.

At a highpoint, he took a moment to look back. He spotted a movement. A figure.

Someone followed. They stopped when they saw him watching. Not hiding but coming no closer.

He walked until the last light touched the tops of the canyons. He'd gathered dry sticks and brush for the fire nest, but not enough for the night fire. He picked a campsite carefully. A place with a wall for the fire to reflect light and warmth.

Flat ground.

Soft and sandy.

He took a juniper limb and swept the ground, clearing prickers and sharp plants from his bed.

The girl arrived just as the fire had caught. She carried firewood. Like him, scavenged from the trail.

She approached quietly, dragging her feet once to make sure he knew she was there.

She dropped the kindling, but the boy saw she still held a length of carved wood. He knew it belonged to a spindle whorl, used for thread or cord. Her sling bulged with the shape of a pot. The stone whorl likely inside.

Just as it had been his time to leave, so it was hers.

She crouched and removed the sling, placing it carefully at a distance from the fire—laying down the spindle. She rose and went to gather more wood. They had walked late, but the night would be longer.

The dark gave way to dawn as if unsure it wanted to leave. The boy and girl cleaned up their camp and ate simply—dried meat and part of a pinon cake that the girl softened with a little water. They drank from pockets in the stone where rainwater still lingered, then set off.

The boy strode with purpose—the girl matching his pace as they headed for the ledge he remembered.

The canyons had been empty since leaving the cliff dwellings. That was good. More people meant more hunters—and less space to plant their small crops. He was watchful as they moved, searching for signs of game or places that might hold enough moisture for their corn.

He caught himself for a moment. Their corn. No words had passed, but he had accepted that the girl was now part of this way forward—as fixed now in his mind as the ledge they walked toward. He watched her move—graceful and sure-footed over the uneven ground. Hair tied back, her clothing softened by use, barefooted like him. Around her neck she wore a carcanet. A simple strip of hide that carried a bright stone.

The land ahead dipped slightly, and they entered a shallow wash. A breeze stirred soft at first, then caught—whipping up a sudden spiral from the ground. Dust and dried seed husks rose and spun, circling in a thin, whirling column.

The girl stepped back as it passed, her eyes following its path. One husk brushed her cheek, then settled gently at her feet. The boy bent and picked it up, handing it to her—a gift from the canyon, as if to say: *welcome. You are part of this too.*

The moon peeked over the east wall as they neared the alcove, their destination. A thin crescent, offering only a sliver of light. Their eyes had adjusted to the dark as the sun left, and they could make out the ledge clearly in the half-light.

The two granaries stood just as the boy remembered. A handful of carved steps cut into the rock, easing a path up the steep face that led onto the rock shelf. The boy turned and took the girl's hand, and they walked forward together.

WALL HOUSE

Home carved from stone and time

THERE WAS ONLY ONE access point to their ledge, and it was narrow—less than the width of the spear from the boy's atlatl.

Past the entrance, the alcove widened. It ran forty paces before narrowing again. Overhead, a rock roof hung low, almost to the cliff edge, the undercut cave pressed into the back wall where it sloped to meet the ground.

The boy walked to the lip of the shelf and dropped a small stone. He counted one finger, two, three—before it struck the canyon floor.

This was a safe place.

Protected.

He walked the length of the alcove, eyes on the seep that dripped—slow and persistent. It was past the end of the ledge, but the boy saw a narrow platform covered in verdant ferns. He could reach it, if he was willing to make the jump.

The girl had opened one of the granaries, moving a small seal stone set in place to close the stone storage bin. About a dozen corn cobs lay scattered in the bottom—dry, shriveled, but intact.

The granaries were the only structures, but stone had been carried up—perhaps enough to begin a one-room dwelling.

She called to the boy and pointed. Soot blackened the cave roof, and ashes lay in a forgotten fire ring. A half-burned black log lay in the center—undisturbed, it seemed since before she was born. Hunters had kept provisions and likely camped here. But they would be the first to settle. It would do.

The boy returned from the seep. He had made the leap, and now his pot was set—slowly filling with clear water that dripped through a crack in the rocks.

As he walked back to the granaries, something caught his eye. A lower level he'd missed before, with his eyes fixed on the dripping water. It was a small shelf—wide enough for four people at most.

He stepped down.

A bone chisel rested beside a shallow depression in the earth.

A sipapu—unfinished.

He crouched and ran his fingers along the indent.

He could finish it.

Make the connection.

Call the ancestors to this place.

They spent the first night with a small fire, finishing the last remains of their travel food. Tomorrow they would explore their canyon. Search for places where the squash and corn might grow—

look for game trails that would tell the story of the animals that they could hunt.

The boy spoke of the sipapu and how one day they might build a kiva and invite the ancestors to receive their thanks.

The girl smiled, sipping the water that tasted pure and cool.

Following the boy had been a risk, but here they were—together, already speaking of a kiva and a house.

She reached into her sling and pulled out a stone.

It matched the one already hanging at her neck—nearly identical in shape and hue.

The boy could see she was working it with a bone tool, carving the channel so it could thread like hers.

He was surprised when she pointed to his neck.

She held it between thumb and forefinger, its fulgent surface reflecting the dancing light of the fire's flames.

She wanted him to wear it one day.

One day, when it was finished.

Early next morning, they descended to the canyon floor. The girl carried seeds for planting. The boy held tight to the atlatl, eyes low for tracks then rising—scanning for movement.

The sun had not yet reached the canyon rim, but there was light enough. He saw signs of hare, and other small game. A recent flood had swept through a wash—mud still soft beneath their feet. The tracks were fresh enough to read, but old enough to tell him the animals had moved on.

They spread out as they moved—boy to the left, girl to the right.

They found places where corn had grown once.

The soil was richer, here and there.

It would need water.

But they had that. And perhaps the boy could shape small channels, help the seep reach some of these beds.

They would need more places like this—if they were to grow enough.

His mind was on squash and corn when he saw the track.

He squatted low, holding his hand just above it, gauging the size of the paw.

Four large toes.

Claws retracted.

A deep imprint, that spoke to the age and weight of the beast.

A long tail.

The freshest sign he'd seen all day.

He rose slowly and began to follow the direction the animal had taken, each step careful.

The girl fell in behind him, close now—wanting them to stay together if the silent hunter still watched.

They moved carefully, as one. The boy's eyes scanned ahead, then down, then ahead once more. He saw a scatter of disturbed ground, the soft roll of torn brush, a flicker of fur half-buried beneath leaves and grit.

A fresh kill.

The long tail had eaten, then covered what remained.

A young deer. The flanks stripped, and the rest hidden beneath a rough pile of soil and stone. The cat would return.

The boy didn't touch it.

He looked at the scene, the way his father had taught him. *What had happened, how long ago, what it meant.*

The animal would be close.

He was about to back away when the girl stepped forward. She placed a pebble she'd found earlier beside the kill. A pure white stone washed clean and round by water. A pretty bibelot she'd intended for their home.

Now it served another purpose—an offer of respect.

The boy looked back toward their ledge. To the seep that gave them water. That would give water to the long tail when there was no rain.

He pictured the narrow entry to the shelf where they would build. He would raise a wall, tight to the rock with a single small doorway—all the way to the cliff edge.

That is how their home became the wall house.

TAPESTRY

Our passage marked by ages

THE SMALL HERD grazed on grasses and bitterbrush, ever watchful.

The boy was downwind but there was no cover to approach.

He would wait.

Hidden.

Let the bighorns come to him.

Five animals—young males cast out from the main herd. Today, he believed the hunt was in his favor.

He had come far from the wall house tracking the sheep. Once he had them in sight, he stopped counting time—and wandered deeper still.

He was far into unfamiliar country.

The sheep moved surefooted across steep rock, the boy stayed as close as he dared.

One animal lagged behind.

It looked weaker than the rest.

His decision made, the boy stood in a half crouch, took two quick steps, and loosed the spear from his atlatl.

Too late.

His movement had spooked the herd. Even the slower animal flinched as the others startled.

The spear sailed just wide, grazing the bighorn's coat before crashing into the rock behind—shattering the sharpened point.

The sheep were gone—heads high, sand kicked up from their cloven hooves, as they fled the canyon floor.

The boy had been holding his breath. As he rose to full height, he let it out in a sharp exhale.

He crossed to where the spear had struck, knelt, and picked it up—ruefully eyeing the ruined point.

For a moment, he stood still, breathing deeply to steady his thoughts and slow his racing heart. This was an unfamiliar place, yet it felt like so many others in the labyrinth of gulches that folded through the canyons—an endless maze of silence and stone.

As he turned to begin the trek toward home his gaze lifted—and caught a shimmer of color on a rock face. A pale band zig zagged across the stone calling to him. He moved toward it slowly, rounding a corner. Then he stopped. Before him stretched a tapestry wall— painted figures and symbols, ancient and alive in the light.

He approached cautiously, taking time to consider each image. The ochres varied—no two the same. Shapes emerged—people and animals, prints of hands and feet, a warrior, who like the boy, carried a weapon.

He stood, watching the wall—memorizing the shapes, the animals. Wondering who had painted here, long ago. At last, he turned and began the long walk home.

Big horn sheep and painted walls filled his thoughts. As he neared their home, he began to wonder how he would tell the girl that today, there was no meat.

Then—a sudden burst from the brush. A turkey exploded into half flight, wings flailing as it rose in alarm. Too fast and too far for the boy to fire his broken spear.

Instinct told the boy to pause.

He followed the turkey tracks, easing through the undergrowth, to see where it had come from.

There.

The nest.

A clutch of eggs, hidden in the shadows. Not meant to be found.

He crouched low, hands steady. There were more, but he chose only three. Enough for a meal, not too many to be missed. He whispered his thanks and covered the nest.

The girl turned the eggs gently in the ash of the fire, careful that each side shared its time with the heat. Thin wisps of steam curled from the shells. After a while, she nodded, and the boy cracked one against a flat stone, peeling back the brittle skin. They ate slowly—one for each of them. The third, saved in its shell for the morning.

He had spoken of the hunt as they ate, but as they relaxed beside the firelight—its glow painting the back of the alcove in orange and red—his thoughts returned to the tapestry wall. Quietly, he began to speak of the painted figures and the stories they seemed to tell.

The boy described the circles that grew smaller and smaller inside one another—the three sided shapes, the figures and animals. He spoke of a beast with a shaggy head, heavy horns, and curved, powerful shoulders. He wondered if it had ever lived or was it only a memory.

The girl had listened carefully, eyes on the fire. But when he spoke of the beast with the shaggy head, she stirred. Her story began with a single word: *once.*

Once the beasts were plentiful. Their herds roamed the plateau, moving like great shadows across the land. Feeding and moving and feeding again.

Some of the people moved with them. The animals did not fear those who followed. At times, they would take one—an old animal, or one left behind by the herd. The beasts were full of meat, and their hides were warm in the night.

In some seasons the herds moved north—seeking cooler places where green grasses still grew. And those who followed left with them.

One year, they didn't return. No beasts, no people, no meat, no hides.

The mesas had grown dry, and the animals needed more than they could give. It was the same for the people who lived high on the plateau. They grew hungry when the crops didn't grow—when the rains no longer came.

Now the rains fell on the mountains.

The girl took a stick and poked the fire. It flared back into life, the flames dancing, orange and yellow.

When the rain moved to the mountains, it still flowed into the canyons. The people gave thanks to the ancestors and left their earth houses on the mesa.

They made their homes in the cliffs.

Perhaps one day the rains will return.

And the shaggy beasts with them.

The boy looked out at the narrow sky between the canyon walls. There was no moon—only stars, bright and strong.

As he watched, a quick line of white flashed across the night.

He closed his eyes to remember it and saw its brightness again.

POTS

Vessels capture what fingers let go

THE SUN DIPPED to touch the canyon rim, painting the rock in a deep unfamiliar color.

The boy watched. Something was strange, different.

He could hold his gaze on the sun's shape—the brightness muted, somehow dimmed. The color deepened to ochre, as if the light itself had thickened.

He remembered the circles he had seen on the tapestry wall, many seasons before, and wondered if this is what the people had drawn.

The air held fine particles—like looking through water, when a fish stirs the stream bed, and the world goes soft with haze.

As the red orb fell from sight, he turned to the wall above him. The shadow crept slowly higher, the last sunlight retreating, chased by the dark.

By the next morning, smoke had settled onto the ledge of the wall house and hung thickly down to the canyon floor. It stifled the air.

The fires were burning somewhere—strong and relentless, scorching the land and blackening the trees.

Perhaps they were close. Perhaps not.

It didn't matter.

The girl and the child moved slowly across the alcove, taking short breaths to keep the burning smoke from their throats.

The girl lifted the water pot. She drank, then passed it to the child.

The child grasped it with both hands, drinking deeply, the water spilled over the rim and down the sides. The pot, now slick and heavy, slipped from the child's grip.

It seemed to fall slowly before striking the rock floor—the crash sharp and final.

Smashed to fragments.

The water, darkening the ground.

The child stood still, frozen in place.

The girl moved to give comfort, but the boy was angry.

Why had she given the pot to the child?

What would they do with only one?

The child clung to her, arms tight around her legs, crying out for the broken jar.

The girl spoke.

A word to the child.

A word to the boy.

Hush.

The time was already past.

The girl had pigments—collected for color.

There was good clay in the wet places of the canyon.

They would build a kiln.

The boy would build a kiln.

And the girl would make the pots.

By late evening, the wind had shifted. The smoke lifted from the canyon, cleared from their home.

The boy sat, the child on his lap—held loosely. He moved his knees in a soft rhythm, and the child smiled.

The anger was gone. The apology was not withheld.

The sharpened stick broke the earth easily.

The boy chose ground with a slight slope for the trench. He worked steadily—breaking the surface with the stick, then scooping the loosened earth with a curved bone.

He dug the kiln three hand widths deep and lined it with stones, set close for even heat.

The girl returned with clay, carried in a deerskin bag.

The child rode comfortably on her back, cradled in a wood framed pack.

She sat nearby and began to coil pots, as the boy lit the fire for the kiln. He added animal dung and the shards of the broken pot for insulation.

He watched her work—steady and sure—as the pots grew taller beneath her hands.

She laid the thin coils in tight spirals, smoothing them as she went.

There were three.

Two tall and delicate.

One, small—shaped for the child. Its thick clay rings might withstand a fall to the ground.

When she finished, the pots stood, smooth-sided, patterned with a glazed design that would fire white and black.

The pots sat in the kiln until the girl gave the signal.

Then he covered them with the earth he had readied, quenching the air—ensuring the black designs would set cleanly against the pale clay.

The girl nodded, it was done and done well.

STONES AND CORN

On stony ground, the seed remembers the hand that placed it

THE SMALL CIRCULAR BUILDING sat on its own ledge—just below the main level of the wall house alcove. The boy poured a trickle of water from his bowl into dry clay, mixing until it darkened and clung to his fingers.

He set the mortar for a new stone.

The rock settled, its weight pressing out a thin rim of clay. He pulled it smooth with quick hands, leaving faint ridges from his fingers in the fresh plaster—marks that would harden with the wall, hidden but lasting, part of the kiva now.

Below, the shadow of a bird slid along the canyon floor, silent and swift. The boy's eyes followed for a moment, before settling on the piles of stone he'd left at the base of the cliff.

He collected rocks and hauled them to the ledge every day—sometimes in his hands, sometimes in a sling. Other times, the girl would fill a skin shaped to hold the stones, and he would raise it from the canyon floor. They needed stones for more granaries, for the kiva—and someday, perhaps, another room in the house.

This was work for times when other work could wait—when water was caught from the seep, meats dried, their skins made ready for clothing or covering.

He looked up. The girl was ready to leave, the child safe in the pack on her back.

He rubbed his hands until the wet mortar dried then crumbled away as sand and then dust.

Standing, he joined her to descend for a day of checking corn.

They followed the narrow path, moving in single file, stepping carefully down the carved steps and into the wide gulch between the canyon walls.

They walked their familiar trail.

The boy checked his snare lines, while the girl checked the planting beds that stretched through the labyrinth of crevices and gullies within a half day's walk of their cliff home. She pressed her finger, feeling for damp, and counting the days until the corn or squash would be ready to harvest.

A hare, taken from a trap, lay snug and lifeless in the sling across the boy's back. Together they walked the rows, pulling weeds that grew too close, tending the plants that would be choked in a season without them.

They were close to the last planting when the girl stopped. Footprints broke the regular surface of the bed, scattered through the soft earth.

The boy crouched, studying the marks.

One person.

Larger. Heavier than the boy.

He glanced up. The child was sleeping, and the girl was silent.

At the edge of the bed, he scanned the ground.

A heel print in the dust where the row ended. Loose soil clinging to a rock beyond marked the way.

The boy straightened, shifting the hare in his sling.

The girl's eyes followed the prints away from the terrace.

They stepped off the row together, following.

The boy led, picking his way up the gully—placing each step with care, moving as quietly as he could.

Wary, but needing to know.

Who? Where?

They turned a bend. Ahead, the trail ended at a steep rock wall.

Their gaze lifted. In the shadow of a cliff house a figure stood.

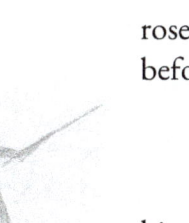

He had watched them approach. Now he rose to full height, legs splayed—a round shield before him, an atlatl stretched wide to the side.

Their eyes locked.

The warrior opened his mouth, thrusting his tongue past teeth and lips.

A signal.

Challenge. Ownership. Defiance.

The boy's hand dropped to his side. His fingers closing on the heavy stone hammer he kept for the killing blow.

The girl's hand found his before he could lift it.

Wait.

Her hand stayed on his.

The warrior did not move, tongue still protruding.

A warm wind breathed down from the mesa, carrying the dry smell of sage. Somewhere beyond, its echo moved through the canyon, fading as the gust passed.

They stepped back, slow and steady, eyes remained locked.

At last, he was gone from view and they turned for home. The boy's hand held firm.

That night on the alcove, the moon dimmed and brightened through passing clouds—the boy and girl sat, their feet close to the fire. The girl reached into the fold in her clothes and pulled a bright stone, a thin strip of hide creating a carcanet that matched the one she wore.

She passed it to the boy.

A gift given and accepted.

In the terraces the corn stood in rows.

Beside the kiva the stones waited.

SKY AND STARS

Earth abides as heavens soar

AS DARKNESS SETTLED on the wall house, the moon traced its slow arc, then dropped beyond the canyon to some other place, some other world.

The first stars appeared above, and the girl and boy ate their meal, warmed on a small fire. The night still held the heat of the day, and the boy let the embers burn away until they were gone to ash.

The dark closed in, and their world became the alcove, the rock walls, and the sky.

They lay together, heads close to the ledge's edge, their shoulders touching—looking up, past the overhang to the sky above.

They strained to see as much sky—and as many stars—as they could, between the rock walls that narrowed their view.

The boy wondered how the stars did not fall. Even small stones dropped from the cliff fell to the ground.

The girl remembered that the sky was the inside of a great bowl, turned upside down to keep it from collapsing into this world.

Above that curve lay another place, its rivers and forests hidden from sight. In its center was a hole—a sipapu. The stars were the light from the fires of its people, shining through the cracks in their floor.

Just as the ancestors had climbed up from the last world, so was it possible to rise to the next. From the high places, people reach toward the sipapu—through that dark place to the ground above—and pull themselves through.

In the next world, animals did not fear people, and the people did not remember hunger. Food grew where it wished, and water never ran dry.

The air was clear—cool in the morning, and warm in the day. The sun and rain changed places often, and the people gave thanks to the ancestors.

It was possible to reach the next world, but only if the world below was cared for and you took your stories with you. The worlds before could not be left in ruin, or the people of the next world would close the sipapu and cover the cracks that let you see their fires.

The boy's gaze lingered on the stars. He imagined the fires above and the people gathered around them, telling stories of the world below. He nodded once, quietly certain, as if he'd seen it for himself.

CEREMONY

What comes before shall yet remain

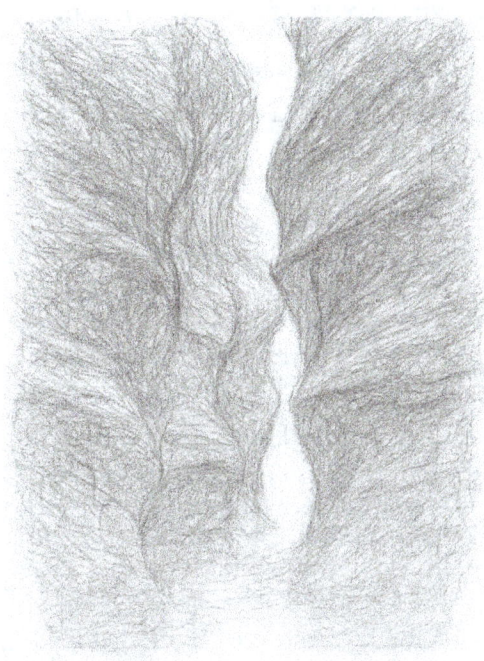

HIS LIPS TOUCHED the seep trickling from a crack in the rock—a drip of moisture that wet his mouth but didn't quench his thirst.

It was the day before the solstice, and the fast had begun.

The girl gathered wood for the kiva and the child helped—stacking it neatly, beside the curved walls of the small building.

Preparations complete, they headed to the canyon floor. They would walk—no work today, time to reflect.

To remember.

To listen to the thoughts of the ancestors who had climbed from the last world so long ago.

They followed the wash into a side canyon. The wall rose higher with each bend, drawing close until they stepped into the narrow shade of the slot.

The low winter light reached only the top bands of rock—ribbons of weak sunlight softening the stone to dull shades of yellow and pink.

The air was still, and they stopped for a moment feeling more than hearing the quiet of the place.

The boy was no stranger here. Once he'd followed a mule deer—its flank pierced by his spear as it limped to escape him—seeking refuge but finding only the long peace. Today he gave thanks for the life that had fed his family.

The girl walked—a hand brushing the wall, feeling the smoothness of the sculpted rock.

The child crouched low to the sandy floor. Picking at pebbles, polished by floods that filled such tight spaces so easily. At last finding one fine enough to keep.

In time, they left the slot and wandered back through the winding canyon until the sky opened above them.

The boy felt the hunger—steady and hollow.

As shadows lengthened on the cliff wall, he rested on the rock floor of the alcove. The girl prepared food for herself and the child, keeping it apart from where the boy lay.

He stilled his thoughts, breathing long and deep.

Tomorrow he would enter the kiva.

At first light the boy rose.

The girl and child were already awake, watching him without speaking.

The kiva stood ready.

Its floor sunk low, closer to the last world, its roof open to the sky to release smoke that would call to the ancestors.

The boy climbed down the ladder with branches of pinon, juniper, and sage. He stepped onto the packed earth floor where a small fire ring waited.

He sparked a fire into life—juniper first, its sharp scent rising with the heat. Then pinon, slower burning, the resin sweetening the smoke. The sage he set aside.

Cross-legged on the floor, he watched the first threads of smoke drift upwards.

The sage would come last—when he called to the ancestors.

The boy closed his eyes.

The hunger was no longer sharp; it sat deep in his belly—his limbs heavy, his mind heavier still.

He breathed in the juniper, the pinon, letting the heat work into his bones.

The flames bent and swayed, sending light across the curved walls, the plaster marked by the faint ridges of his fingers.

He thought of the girl and the child outside. Of the ancestors who had walked the last world searching for the sipapu—a way into this world.

He placed sage on the coals.

A new smoke rose—thin, blue-grey, carrying its sweetness upward, through the opening in the roof. It curled and lingered before slipping away.

The walls began to shift. Shapes formed in the flickering light: hunters striding with spears, women shaping clay, the dark mouths of other kivas, in other canyons, smoke drifting from their roofs.

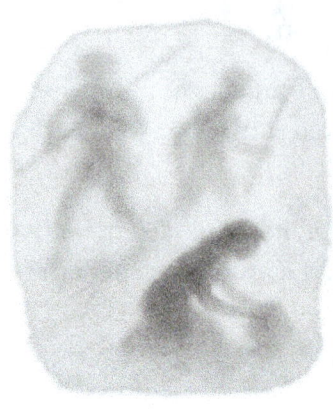

The sound of voices filled his ears; they spoke as they worked, grinding corn and chipping stones to sharpen the edges into points.

Beyond, he heard another voice—the girl speaking to the child.

She told of a world where stories were forgotten. Where the people cared for themselves but not for the land, or for the animals. The rain no longer fell, and the crops refused to grow.

And the people.

The people fought over what remained.

Only a few had found the sipapu and climbed to this world. The few who remembered the stories, who would care for the new land, begin again, and hold fast to what had been lost.

The old world was sealed—no one could climb out, and no one could go back.

Only the spirits would come with the ceremony—welcomed by the men in the kivas.

The girl's voice faded but its meaning held.

The boy saw the few, the ancestors, who had climbed through the sipapu—the hole between the worlds---carrying jars of water, bundles of seeds.

The air trembled with their footfalls, the stone ringing as their ladders struck the ground.

He reached for them, but it was too late. They faded away with the final wisps of smoke from the untended fire at his feet.

What remained was the slow rise of his chest, and the steady pulse of his heart.

PICTOGRAPHS

Pictures tell a story the rocks have heard before

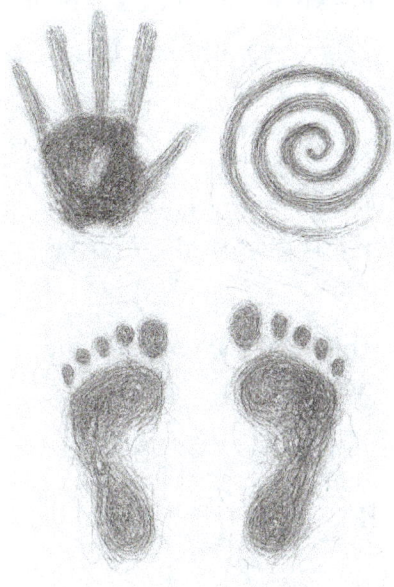

THE STRANGE RED-HOODED BIRD, wings lifted high as if
shrugging, watched from an overhanging rock. The boy knew there
must be a kill near—perhaps a long tail was feeding, or a pack of
coyotes.

He moved easily, at one with the ground as it shifted from sand
to stone, and then back to sand. Earlier, he'd seen the cat's tracks. It
was no threat—only another part of his world.

He walked toward his old cliff home. Not too far from the wall
house, but far enough to check his markers.

Many seasons ago he had set stones—one atop another, balanced
just so—to say: *you are on the path, this is the way.*

Sometimes he checked them.

Once, an animal had knocked one loose. Another time, a third rock appeared above his two. But no people had come.

Back at the alcove the girl knelt with the child beside her.

She ground the pigments—red ochre from the cliff vein, soft yellow from a crumbling ledge, and black soot scraped from the roof of their home.

Each she mixed with water from the gourd, stirring the colors with a stout willow twig. *A smear of sap from the firepot bound the colors.*

They deepened as they blended, darkening in the shifting light, carrying the scent of earth and smoke.

The child watched closely, as if learning a ceremony.

The boy gave two sharp whistles as he climbed the carved steps to the wall house.

I am here, are we ready?

They had chosen a wall at the end of the ledge—clear of the smoke from the house or the kiva, protected from the sun and rain by the overhang of the cliff above.

The girl pressed her palm into the red ochre, the color filling the lines and whorls of her skin. She placed it flat against the stone; the print stood out clean and bright. Satisfied, she added her other hand, the right just slightly higher.

Beside her, the child giggled as the boy dipped both small feet into the yellow, then lifted them high. He raised the child to the wall, pressing each foot in turn until two bright tracks stood side by side.

At last, the boy dipped his fingers into the black. With slow, steady strokes, he painted a spiral that wound inward, small at the center, as if drawing the eye to another place.

When it was done, he sat back.

The marks glowed against the pale stone—hand, foot, and spiral—three signs bound together.

Long after their voices faded, the marks would remain, holding the memory of this moment against the stone.

From below the sound of people carried into the alcove—a woman's laughter, and a man's deeper reply.

They called out, reaching up to the ledge, then appeared a moment later, climbing the faint steps from the canyon floor.

The boy stood. It was his sister, and with her, the man she had chosen.

She met his eyes—the seasons between them closing in a heartbeat.

The man said nothing at first. He gave a short nod, his gaze moving from the house to the granaries, to the kiva, and finally, to the marks on the wall.

The boy moved to join him, and the girl took the hand of the sister and joined it with the child.

They had brought pots and tools, setting them beside the kiva before sitting cross-legged, as if weighing the space.

No words yet—only the wind curling along the cliff face, and a canyon crow cawing and circling, riding the thermals from the heat of the rock.

That night they shared food by the fire.

Stories came slowly at first, but each one gradually stitched the seasons apart into a single cloth.

As the flames sank to embers, the boy looked at the wall.

In the shifting light, the hand, the feet, and the spiral seemed to pulse with their own life.

The boy placed a hand on the belly of the girl, feeling the quiet life within.

His sister was here. They were bound to this ledge, their lives written into the stone.

Soon they would be six.

ANCESTRAL PUEBLOANS

THE PEOPLE we now know as Ancestral Puebloans flourished for centuries across the American Southwest, particularly on the high mesas and canyons of Colorado Plateau.

Just over a thousand years ago, they began building the cliff dwellings for which they are best remembered—stone homes set deep in alcoves, forcing us to wonder at the reasons for choosing these secure, elevated locations.

Archaeologists believe that these cliff homes were only occupied for a century or so before being abandoned.

It is uncertain why they left, but prolonged drought, resource depletion, and pressure from neighboring groups are among the leading theories that shaped their migration.

These pressures are not unique to ancient peoples. In many ways they remain part of the human condition.

In my work, these themes sit at the center, molding characters as they respond to change, scarcity, and elements often beyond their control.

The American Southwest remains an inspiring landscape of canyons, mesas and wide-open sky. Places like Mesa Verde and Chaco Canyon offer glimpses into how Ancestral Puebloans adapted to harsh, beautiful environments, while countless smaller, lesser-known sites lie hidden in remote canyons. It was these quiet remnants—that inspired Ancient Ones.

ABOUT THE AUTHOR

TIMOTHY HARGREAVES grew up between the rolling countryside of Cheshire—where rural fields meet the industrial north-west—and the stark, sodden beauty of England's Lake District. There, he spent more time in the worlds of Arthur Ransome, Henry Treece, and C.S. Lewis than doing his homework.

For over two decades, Tim worked shaping guest experiences in the Colorado Rockies, including the complete redevelopment of an iconic ski lodge/condominium hotel. After years helping others connect with the mountains, he turned inward, writing fiction rooted in land, memory, and transformation.

A former contributor to Vail Magazine, he lives in the Colorado high country, where the forest meets his back door and wildlife—deer, bear, bobcats, and the occasional mountain lion—passes through.

Follow Timothy Hargreaves

Facebook:

@timothyhargreavesbooks

Goodreads: https://www.goodreads.com/author/show/58453207.

Website: www.timothyhargreaves.com